Snowcone:
The Sociopath's Dog

By Robert Maxwell Gibson

Illustrated by Melissa Doskotz

For Aunt Bette and Uncle Jeffrey

Snowcone was a good dog.
It was time for his walk.
Snowcone hated walks.

Snowcone's owner was not so good.
He was a sociopath.
And he didn't carry a poop bag.

Down at the park, dogs must be leashed.
Dogs were not leashed.
Except Snowcone.

Snowcone wondered why the other dogs did not take off.
Perhaps a non-murderous owner made domestic life more attractive.
Still, how much better could their owners be?
The sign clearly said, "Dogs must be leashed."

Snowcone's owner started talking to a lady on the bench.
A perfect candidate to bring home and murder.
"Run! Run for your life!" yelled Snowcone.

"Looks like Snowcone got jealous that I was paying attention to you."
"Isn't he the sweetest thing?"
"Don't fall for his wiles. Kick him in the shins.
We could both escape."

She did not heed Snowcone's warning.

She would become another victim unless Snowcone could enlist some help.

"You lot. If you could free my leash from his grip, then I could foil his vile scheme."

Snowcone caught the interest of a few of the dogs.
One replied, "Bark. Bark bark bark."
"You fool. Now is a time for action. Saying 'bark' is as worthless as it is meaningless."

Upon returning home, the lady promptly accepted a drink.
Snowcone regretted drinking from her water bottle in the park.
"Hurry. Follow me. You don't have much time left."

The lady downed the drink in one long swig.
"Tonight should be fun."
"Fun? Fetch is fun. Murder is evil."
The lady ignored him and sniffed, "Smells good. Is that bacon?"
She headed back toward the kitchen. A lost cause.

A ring from the doorbell pierced through the alluring odor.
Snowcone rushed to the door. Hope renewed.
"Stand back. I'm going to make a run for it as soon as the door opens."
Apparently Snowcone had never thought of this strategy of escape before now.

Snowcone's owner scooped him up before answering the door.
"Vote for Smith. He'll clean up the streets."
"But he makes the mess in the house!" Snowcone informed the stranger.
"Unless you're referring to me, and I still think a poop bag is the best solution."

A crash from the kitchen cut the campaigning short.
"Whoops. I should go check on that. Thanks for the information."
"Don't give up your pitch! Get your foot in the door! I can hop over it."
More pressing, though, was how the next house over would vote.

The lady had gone for the bacon.
Instead she got a skillet to the face as the drugs took effect.
The two most common uses of the skillet at once for the first time.
The downside being a floor covered with bacon. Depending on whom you asked.

Snowcone rushed to the backyard and dug furiously near the fence.
He might just have enough time to escape while she was finished off.
The bacon would still be good cold.

"Snowcone. How many times have I told you to dig in the middle of the yard?"
His first few shovels of dirt were relocated in Snowcone's hole.
Snowcone tried to return the favor with little success.

"Look at you. Your paws are all dirty.
Guess I'll have to give you a bath."
"Why not leave me on the street? Smith can take care of it."

During Snowcone's bubble bath, a storm overtook the house.
Thunder boomed. The walls shook from the wind.
Once clean, Snowcone retreated to under the bed, where he shook as well.

By the time the storm ended, Snowcone's owner was fast asleep.
Snowcone ventured through the doggie door to the backyard.
The thunder had knocked down a single slat from the fence.
Snowcone still felt that this boon alone did not justify thunder's existence.

Snowcone could fit through the hole.
He wanted to bring evidence as well.
His bubble bath had been for nothing.

Snowcone's excavation landed him a femur.
Not ideal for his size, but he wanted to hurry to the police.
Dogs are extremely shortsighted it seems.

Snowcone soon discovered that the bone did not fit through the slot in the fence.
Snowcone persisted until he had banged the fence enough to expand the hole.
Turning the bone probably helped too.

Snowcone knew of a police station that was not too far.
The journey seemed to go on forever in the tense silence of the night.
The streets were full of fallen branches from the storm.
Snowcone might vote "Smith" yet.

The police had little else to do at this time of morning other than tend to Snowcone.
"My, that's quite the bone you've got there.
Let me have a look."

"Only a real loving owner would get such a great bone for his dog.
Let me have a look at your tag and we can reunite you."
"What? No! Your assumptions are misplaced."

"Steady on there...uh...Snowcone. You can have your bone back.
The little ones always seem to be the most possessive."
"I don't want the bone. I want you to look at it.
And consider going back to school for some extra anatomy."

"Hello sir. I found your dog wandering about and came to return him."
"Snowcone, you mischievous little thing. Thank you so much, officer."
"Not at all. This happens quite often after storms."
Snowcone felt his fear of storms was justified with this information.

"Is that bacon I smell?
I'm tempted to invite myself inside. But I already had a donut.
I suppose I'll just be on my way. Have a nice day."
"That's it? You're not going to question him?
At least remember to mention the bone in the police report."

"Snowcone you're a naughty little thing. I can't stay mad at you, though.
How about a tummy rub?"
Snowcone's owner rubbed his tummy. His leg began to run.
"Curse you. Today's walk will be different. Just you wait."

Robert Maxwell Gibson is an independent videogame developer whose most recent game is *Upside Kitty*. After a long hiatus from his middle school comic strip, he decided it was time to return to writing. He is currently living in Seattle and looking for dry tennis courts.

Melissa Doskotz is a born and bred New Yorker, hailing from Stony Brook, Long Island. She has been drawing since she could hold a crayon and has been drawing and painting ever since. When she "grew up" she eventually went on to study art at the Fashion Institute of Technology and graduated with a BFA in Illustration. Today she lives in Orland Florida where she continues to work on numerous illustration projects and sculptures.

www.ingramcontent.com/pod-product-compliance
Lightning Source LLC
Chambersburg PA
CBHW070356130626
46556CB00007B/3189

Stephen and Tiffany Domena

SOMEONE COVETS YOU

An Allegory That Exposes The Subliminal Battles Of Our Lives

SOMEONE COVETS YOU

An Allegory That Exposes Subliminal Battles In Our Lives

By: Stephen and Tiffany Domena

Published by Mandatory Success Publishing at Smashwords

Mandatory Success Visions

ISBN-13:
978-0692266298

ISBN-10:
0692266291